PLAYS FOR PERFORMANCE

A series designed for
contemporary production and study
Edited by
Nicholas Rudall and Bernard Sahlins

ARISTOPHANES

Lysistrata

In a New Translation by
Nicholas Rudall

Ivan R. Dee
CHICAGO

Library of Congress Cataloging-in-Publication Data:
Aristophanes.
[Lysistrata. English]
Lysistrata / Aristophanes ; in a new translation by Nicholas Rudall.
p. cm. — (Plays for performance)
Translation of: Lysistrata.
ISBN 0-929587-61-8 (cloth : alk. paper). —
ISBN 0-929587-57-X (pbk. : alk. paper)
1. Greece—History—Peloponnesian War, 431–404 B.C.—Drama. I. Rudall, Nicholas. II. Title. III. Series.
PA3877.L8 1991
882'.01—dc20 91-17335

INTRODUCTION

by Nicholas Rudall

Aristophanes' *Lysistrata* was performed at Athens in the early spring of the year 411 B.C.E. Aristophanes wrote the play at a time when the Athenian populace must have been in the depths of despair. Apart from a brief truce, the Peloponnesian War was now in its twentieth year, and in 412 B.C.E., just a few months before the performance of *Lysistrata*, Athens had received devastating news. The city had mounted a massive naval and military campaign against the island of Sicily. Now they had learned (an apocryphal story tells us that the information came from a chance remark in a barber shop) that all was lost, the fleet decimated, and thousands of men either captured or killed.

Aristophanes wrote the *Lysistrata* as an immediate and passionate plea to stop the carnage. This plea was not new to him. Some dozen or so years earlier, when he first began to write, he had campaigned against war. After this latest disaster, and with the prospect of unremitting continued slaughter, he renewed his campaign.

To approach a contemporary production of *Lysistrata*, a director should have some basic knowledge of how and why the original play was performed. But it must be said that any attempt to reproduce the original will be impossible. First and foremost, Aristophanic comedy was a *com-*

munal and *ephemeral* event. The play was performed only once and before an audience of Athenians, and it was a response to an immediate and recent catastrophe. Second, it took place at a festival (whether the Lenaea or the Greater Dionysia) dedicated to fertility. At these festivals, Athenians performed rituals which would ensure the survival of themselves as human beings and their city as a political entity. What they saw upon their stage was themselves, threatened by extinction. Comedy's function was to give them the hope that death would die and they would live.

These simple facts are critical for a modern understanding of the play. The central message is a direct and clear exposition of comedy's function within the context of a festival of fertility: If mankind continues to fight, mankind will die. It is of paramount importance for a modern director to recognize that the women of the play are all married (though there is no specific reference to Lysistrata's husband). What the women are saying is, "We will produce no more children for men to use as the fodder of war." This central fact is too often ignored. Too many productions people the stage with scantily clad nymphets. Of course, originally the women's parts were played by men, which compounded the humor and denied any sense of nubile eroticism. Furthermore, since this was a season of fertility, the phallus was to be seen routinely in the streets of Athens. Not only did the Athenians carry phalluses around the city in ribald celebrations, but they were to be seen as sacred adornments on the fronts of houses. It would not have been forgotten that Alcibiades, one of the leaders of the Sicilian expedition, had been accused of breaking off the phalluses from the doorways of hundreds of houses before the disaster. In any case, the phallus is the central symbol of the play. When the women seize the Acropolis, which was the seat of male power and the repository of state funds, the chorus of old men take a battering ram but are unable to break through the double doors of the Acropolis. The ending of the play is equally dependent on phallic imagery. The men of Greece are in a permanent state of erection, and their ambassadors' rods of office, hidden beneath their cloaks, are indistinguishable from the real thing.

Suggestions for a Modern Production

The chorus should be sung or chanted in the versified choral odes. The music should be very simple. If there is any dance it should be equally simple.

It is critical that means be found to reinforce the fact that the women are mothers (strollers, baby carriages, babies in swaddling clothes, etc.).

The phallus in Athens was both sacred and risqué. For a contemporary audience, it is only the latter. The director should therefore make the phallus comic, even grotesque, rather than erotic. The original stage phallus was very large, made of leather, and bright red.

This leads me to the observation that the greatest challenge for a director of *Lysistrata* is to produce a play about fertility and survival rather than sex, frustration, and gratification.

The Translation

Most available translations are written in verse that range in style from prudish Victorianism to suggestive modern lyricism. One of the reasons

Aristophanes' plays survive is that, alone of ancient authors, he used abundant colloquialisms. His language was the living *spoken* language. His plays were presumably used to preserve and teach that language in later centuries. But his style was also a hybrid. For comic effect, he constantly juxtaposed the high styles of tragedy or rhetoric to the commonplace or the obscene. Furthermore, his lyrics were counted among the most exquisite ever written. The translation here attempts to capture these radical changes in stylistic diction. But primarily this is a translation for the stage. It is written to be spoken by actors, not read by students or scholars. It is faithful to the text, but absurdities have been clarified and ancient puns replaced with modern ones.

The immediacy of the disaster in Sicily and its effect upon the community of Athens cannot be recaptured. But what has made the *Lysistrata* one of the greatest plays ever written is its central eternal idea: Peace is survival and a female yearning; war is a male phallic aberration.

CHARACTERS

LYSISTRATA, CALONIKE, MYRRHINE — Athenian women
LAMPITO, a Spartan woman
A BOEOTIAN WOMAN
A CORINTHIAN WOMAN
COMMISSIONER OF PUBLIC SAFETY
KINESIAS, husband of Myrrhine
SPARTAN HERALD AND ENVOYS
CHORUS OF ATHENIAN MEN
CHORUS OF ATHENIAN WOMEN
A BABY
A NURSE

Lysistrata

LYSISTRATA: *(pacing)* Women! *(to audience)* Tell them there's an orgy going on, or a party for Pan, or a fertility rite, and everything stops. You can't get through the streets. Women everywhere with their tambourines. But today there's not one woman here. Sorry! Here's someone. It's my next-door neighbor. Good morning, Calonike!

CALONIKE: Same to you, Lysistrata. But what's the matter? Don't squidge your face up like that, darling. Looking daggers doesn't suit you.

LYSISTRATA: I am on fire. Right down to the bone. I'm furious. And all because of us women. You know what our husbands say. They say we're sly, deceitful, always . . .

CALONIKE: They're right, too.

LYSISTRATA: We promised to meet today to plan something devastatingly important. And what happens? They stay in bed.

CALONIKE: Oh, they'll be along, my sweet. It's so hard to get out of the house. We have to bend over backwards for our husbands, wake the maid, wash the baby, feed the baby, put the baby to bed.

LYSISTRATA: But there are other things far far more important.

CALONIKE: Is that why you're calling the meeting, Lysistrata? How big a thing is this?

LYSISTRATA: It's big.

CALONIKE: And thick?

LYSISTRATA: Massive. It's big enough for all of us.

CALONIKE: Then why aren't they here?

LYSISTRATA: If THAT'S what was up, they'd be here. No, Calonike, this is something I've been tossing around for the last few nights. I couldn't get any sleep.

CALONIKE: Sounds good to me! Was it good?

LYSISTRATA: So good that.... The hope and salvation of Greece depend upon us women.

CALONIKE: On us? Bye-bye, Greece.

LYSISTRATA: We must make the decisions on national and international affairs. Take the Spartan question. Are you for peace or annihilation?

CALONIKE: Annihilation every time.

LYSISTRATA: And the same for the Boeotians?

CALONIKE: *Yes*! ... Wait a minute. NO!! They have marvelous pickled eels in that part of the country.

LYSISTRATA: As for Athens.... It could happen to us ... but I can't bring myself to say it. But listen, if all the women came here, from Boeotia, from Sparta, from the rest of the Peloponnese, we could save the entire country.

CALONIKE: Us? Do you really think *we* could do something practical? All we are good for is sitting in front of the mirror, all primped and flowered in our exquisite little negligees and those chic little oriental slippers.

LYSISTRATA: Exactly! Those are the weapons that will save us—perfumes and rouge, slippers and slips, and those see-through negligees.

CALONIKE: Save us? What do you mean?

LYSISTRATA: The result will be that the men will never raise their spears again....

CALONIKE: Then I'll have my best dress sent to the cleaners....

LYSISTRATA: Nor shoulder their shields ...

CALONIKE: And slip into that little negligee ...

LYSISTRATA: Nor unsheathe their swords ...

CALONIKE: And buy me a pair of those oriental slippers.

LYSISTRATA: Then wasn't it essential for the women to be here?

CALONIKE: Be here? They should have flown like the wind.

LYSISTRATA: Listen, darling, you know what they're like. They're real Athenians: never do today what you can put off till tomorrow. But no one came from the coast, nor from Salamis either.

CALONIKE: Don't worry about them. They'll be here. They'd do anything for a good ride.

LYSISTRATA: And where are the Acharnian women? I thought they'd be here first, after all they've had to put up with in this awful war.

CALONIKE: I saw Theogenes' wife as I was leaving. She was flying over here ... high as a kite already. But look, hey, here's a few coming now. And some more over there. Marvelous. Marvelous. Where are they from?

LYSISTRATA: Pisa, I think.

CALONIKE: Smells like it.

MYRRHINE: Are we late, Lysistrata? Well, why don't you answer?

LYSISTRATA: I am very upset, Myrrhine. You are so late when the matter is so important.

MYRRHINE: I couldn't find my girdle in the dark. *(still pouting)* What's so important?

CALONIKE: Hold on a minute. She'll tell you everything when the Spartans and Boeotians get here.

MYRRHINE: That's all right with me.... Here's Lampito coming for a start.

LYSISTRATA: Welcome, Lampito, you Spartan beauty, you.

CALONIKE: What a healthy complexion!

WOMAN: Throbbing with life.

2ND WOMAN: Ripe as a melon!

3RD WOMAN: She could strangle a bull.

LAMPITO: By golly, I think I could. I do my exercises every day—a few pushups every morning before breakfast.

LYSISTRATA: What a nice pair of titties!

LAMPITO: Keep your hands to yourself. What do you think I am? A sacred cow?

LYSISTRATA: And who is this other little girl? Where is she from?

LAMPITO: She's an aristocratic young lady from Boeotia.

LYSISTRATA: Ah, "Boeotia of the fertile plain."

CALONIKE: *(lifting her robe)* Looks as if someone's been mowing the grass.

LYSISTRATA: And who is this?

LAMPITO: She is from Corinth. Her family is very big back there.

CALONIKE: She's pretty big back here.

LAMPITO: All right. Let's get down to business. Who was it called this meeting?

LYSISTRATA: I did.

LAMPITO: Well, then tell us what you have in mind.

MYRRHINE: Yes, tell us, sweetie, what's so important?

LYSISTRATA: I'll answer you both in a minute. But first I want to ask a little question.

MYRRHINE: Go right ahead.

LYSISTRATA: Do you or do you not crave to have your husbands, the fathers of your children, home beside you? I know that all your husbands are abroad.

CALONIKE: My husband's been gone for the last five months, up in the mountains of Thrace.

MYRRHINE: Mine's been in Pylos for seven.

LAMPITO: My man's no sooner rotated out of the line than he's plugged back in. There's no discharge in this war.

LYSISTRATA: And you can't find a lover anywhere. Not even synthetics. Ever since those Milesians revolted and cut off the leather trade, you can't find one of those eight-inch do-it-yourself kits anywhere in town. So ... if I can provide a plan that would bring an end to this war, I take it that I can count on your support.

CALONIKE: YOU can count on me, and if it's money you need I'd pawn the shift off my back—then we could all go out and get smashed.

MYRRHINE: I'm with you all the way. Even if they take me and split me up the middle and filet me like a mackerel.

LAMPITO: Me, too! I'd climb the highest mountain in Sparta if I could just set my eyes on peace again.

LYSISTRATA: All right, then, I'll tell you. There is no need to keep it a secret any longer. Sisters, women of Greece, if we have any hopes of forcing our husbands to negotiate peace, we must resort to total abstinence.

CALONIKE: From what?

MYRRHINE: Yes, what?

LYSISTRATA: You'll do it?

CALONIKE: Of course we will, even if it kills us.

LYSISTRATA: Very well, then. We must resort to total abstinence from . . . the Prick. Why are you turning away? Where are you going? Hey! Why all this mooching and shaking of heads? *(mock tragic)* Why so pale? Whence these tears? Will you do it or won't you? Well, what are you going to do?

CALONIKE: I just couldn't do it. On with the war!

MYRRHINE: Me neither. On with the war!

ALL: ON WITH THE WAR!

LYSISTRATA: Is that all you have to say, my little mackerel? Two minutes ago you were ready to be split up the middle.

CALONIKE: Got any other ideas? Think of something else. Anything. Look, I'd walk through fire if you told me to, but to give up the the ... thing.... Uh uh. There's nothing like it, Lysistrata.

LYSISTRATA: *(to the Corinthian and the Boeotian)* What about you, and you?

CORINTHIAN: I'd be quite willing to walk through fire.

BOEOTIAN: Me, too. Any fire around?

LYSISTRATA: Whores, the whole lot of you! It's no wonder they write tragedies about us. You're a bunch of Phaedras, that's all you are. You'd jump into bed with anyone. But you, my Spartan friend, if you, just you, join me in this, we can still salvage my plan. Give me your vote.

LAMPITO: It's pretty tough, by golly, for girls to sleep without their dickies, but I'm with you. We need peace so badly.

LYSISTRATA: Oh, you darling! The only woman worthy of the name.

CALONIKE: Well, suppose we did ... well, as far as possible, abstain from ... what you said—God forbid. Could something like that bring peace any sooner?

LYSISTRATA: Good God, of course. All we have to do is lounge around with the right amount of makeup on, maybe a flimsy slip, or nothing at all, and we just slink by them, perfumed and powdered and shaved smooth in all the right places.... Wham! Up they'll go. Lusting for a quick lay. But we won't go near them. Total abstinence. I wouldn't be surprised if they stopped the war within a week.

LAMPITO: It could work. Menelaus dropped his sword when he saw Helen all nekked.

CALONIKE: *(to Lysistrata)* Wait a minute, buddy. What if they just walk away?

LYSISTRATA: Then we'll just have to take things into our own hands.

CALONIKE: There's nothing like the real thing.

BOEOTIAN: What if they grab us and drag us off to the bedroom?

LAMPITO: Hold on to the door.

CORINTHIAN: What if they beat us?

LYSISTRATA: You can give in. But don't enjoy it. Be nasty about it. It's no fun for them when it's no fun for you. It's not copulation without co-operation.

MYRRHINE: I suppose it's all right if the *both* of you agree to this.

LAMPITO: You can be sure of one thing: we Spartan women will make our men do exactly as they're told. But this lot in Athens! You'll never convince these fighting cocks.

LYSISTRATA: We'll take care of it. I know how to make them listen.

LAMPITO: I just don't see how you can make them do it. After all, they have a fleet in the harbor and money in the Acropolis.

LYSISTRATA: That's all taken care of. We're taking over the Acropolis today. The older women are up there already pretending to be holding a sacrifice. They're just waiting until we reach an agreement. As soon as we do, they seize the Acropolis.

LAMPITO: I am very impressed. That's an excellent plan.

LYSISTRATA: Then what are we waiting for? All we have to do now is swear a solemn oath.

CALONIKE: You make the oath, we'll swear to it.

LYSISTRATA: Excellent. This is it. Lampito, give me your shield. No, put it on the ground. Not that way up. Turn it over. Now, has anyone got any spare entrails of lamb?

CALONIKE: What kind of ceremony is this, Lysistrata?

LYSISTRATA: *(scratching her head)* Well, I think it's worked before. Aeschylus used it in the *Seven Against Thebes*. They slaughtered a sheep and swore on a shield ... I think.

CALONIKE: But you can't make an oath about peace on a shield. That would be ridiculous.

LYSISTRATA: Then what do you suggest?

CALONIKE: How about a big white stallion?

LYSISTRATA: Anyone got a spare one?

CALONIKE: I never thought of that.

LYSISTRATA: We're wasting time.

MYRRHINE: I know. First we get an enormous bowl. Then we put it on the ground *(to Lampito)* the right way up. Then we proceed to slaughter a gallon or two of good red wine and swear that ... we won't dilute it with water.

BOEOTIAN: I like that oath.

LYSISTRATA: Bring the bowl and the wine.

CALONIKE: Oooh! Girls! What an enormous bowl! It gives me a thrill just to touch it.

LYSISTRATA: Set it down and place your hands reverently upon this blessed offering to the Gods. *(they raise the wine skin)* O Goddess in Heaven . . .

ALL: O Goddess in Heaven . . .

LYSISTRATA: Our Mistress Persuasion . . .

ALL: Our Mistress Persuasion . . .

LYSISTRATA: And thou, O hallowed skin . . .

ALL: And thou, O hallowed skin . . .

LYSISTRATA: Hear our prayer.

ALL: Hear our prayer.

MYRRHINE: *(jumping up and down)* Oooh! Look at the blood! Look at the blood!

CALONIKE: Excellent bouquet.

MYRRHINE: Let me swear first.

CALONIKE: No, me! Gimme the BOWL!

MYRRHINE: Choose you for it! . . . *(they proceed to play a children's game to see who goes first)*

LYSISTRATA: Lampito, all of you women, come place your right hands on the cup and repeat after me, in order . . . I WILL HAVE NOTHING TO DO WITH HUSBAND OR LOVER.

CALONIKE: I will have nothing to do with husband or lover.

LYSISTRATA: EVEN THOUGH HE COME TO ME WITH A HARD ON. *(pause)* Go on, say it.

CALONIKE: Even though he come to me with a hard on. Ooohhh! Lysistrata, I can't go on with this!

LYSISTRATA: I SHALL REMAIN AT HOME UNMOUNTED.

MYRRHINE: I shall remain at home unmounted.

LYSISTRATA: IN MY THINNEST SAFFRON SILK.

MYRRHINE: In my thinnest saffron silk.

LYSISTRATA: SO THAT HE MAY BECOME ...

MYRRHINE: So that he may become ...

LYSISTRATA: AS STIFF AS A BOARD.

MYRRHINE: *(also forcing herself to say it)* As stiff as a board.

LYSISTRATA: I WILL NOT GIVE MYSELF ...

LAMPITO: I will not give myself ...

LYSISTRATA: WILLINGLY TO MY HUSBAND.

LAMPITO: Willingly to my husband.

LYSISTRATA: AND IF HE TAKES ME BY FORCE ...

LAMPITO: And if he takes me by force ...

LYSISTRATA: I SHALL RESIST HIM AND LIE ABSOLUTELY STILL.

LAMPITO: *(also with difficulty)* I shall resist him and lie absolutely still.

LYSISTRATA: I SHALL NOT LIFT MY SLIPPERS TO THE CEILING.

BOEOTIAN: I shall not lift my slippers to the ceiling.

LYSISTRATA: I SHALL NEVER ASSUME AN ANIMAL POSTURE.

CORINTHIAN: I shall never assume an animal posture.

LYSISTRATA: AND IF I KEEP THIS OATH LET ME DRINK FROM THIS BOWL. *(by this time the five main women have turned their backs on the ceremony, but when they hear this last phrase they rush back and shout together)*

ALL: AND IF I KEEP THIS OATH LET ME DRINK FROM THIS BOWL!

LYSISTRATA: BUT IF I SLIP OR FALTER, LET MY BOWL BE FILLED WITH WATER.

ALL: *(much quieter)* But if I slip or falter, let my bowl be filled with water.

LYSISTRATA: You have all sworn?

CALONIKE: We have. *(she indicates to the women who all shout together)*

ALL: Aah, men.

LYSISTRATA: Well, then, I'll make the sacrifice.

CALONIKE: Not too much now. We want to *stay* friends now, don't we? *(The women gather round and drink. Loud cries backstage.)*

LAMPITO: What's all the commotion?

LYSISTRATA: Just what I told you. The women have seized the Acropolis. The Treasury is OURS. Lampito, rush back to Sparta, get everything in order back there. Leave these girls here as hostages. Leave the rest to us. Girls, into the Acropolis! Shut the gates! Ram the bolts in tight!

CALONIKE: What about the men? Won't they send reinforcements?

LYSISTRATA: That's no problem. Leave them to me. Whether they come with fire or threats and an army, NOTHING will make me open these gates, except on my terms.

CALONIKE: We'll show them. If they're going to call us dirty names, we might as well deserve them.

CHORUS OF OLD MEN *(the parts are designated I through VII)*

Before the doors of the Acropolis. The men are carrying lighted torches and a battering ram.

MAN I: Forward march, Draces, me boy, forget your backs, lads. I know these logs are green and heavy. But to it, boys, to it!

MAN II: What a life! There's this to be said for longevity, you get to see things you never thought you'd see.

MAN III: Hey, Strymodorus, hey! I never thought I'd live to see our women, dammit, seize the citadel.

MAN IV: We gave them everything they needed: food, clothing, and a punch in the mouth. Who'd have thought they'd have barred the doors—all ... the subversive whores!

MAN I: Now, Philourgos, get a move on! To the Acropolis on the double!
We'll pile up the logs in a great big heap,
And set them on fire while they're fast asleep.
We'll try them for treason. We'll cook their goose. And the first to go will by Ly—, Ly— *(remembering)* Lycon's wife....

MAN V: They're not going to make a fool out of me. No, sir! Cleomenes tried it fifty years ago, the stinking old fool!

MAN VI: Oh, we could sniff *him* out all right. He never took a bath for six long years. We flushed that Spartan out of there.

MAN VII: Oh, that was a siege, my friends. Shields to the left of us, shields to the right. I slept like a baby.

MAN I: So what should we do when *women*, of all things, women (whom God and Euripides hate) *women* try the same trick? If we fail to dispose of these hags, I'll turn in the medals I won at *Marathon*.

ALL: Move your feet and tote that load
Just a few more yards of Acropolis road.
Up the step and onto the porch
Drop your burdens and apply the torch!

MAN II: Damn this smoke.

ALL: *(mass coughing and rubbing of eyes)*
We've come to aid the goddess,
We'll save her come what may,
For if the women stay inside,
They'll keep us from our pay.

MAN II: Damn this smoke!

MAN I: Well, thanks be to God, we made it. The fire is bright and burning. Here's my plan of attack. First we'll take a torch, light it in the fire, and then use it as a battering ram.... No, that wouldn't work. Well, if they don't listen to us and throw open the gates, we'll set fire to the woodwork and smoke them out. Damn this smoke! At ease, men. There's a logistical problem here. What we really need is an army of foreign advisers to take over the siege. All right, men, light the sacred fire. "Victory sits on our helm!"

ALL: BURN THE BITCHES WHO CAPTURED THE CAPITOL. DEATH TO THE WOMEN, VICTORY FOR MEN!

CHORUS OF OLD WOMEN *(parts designated as for the Old Men)*

WOMAN I: Come on, girls, I smell fire and smoke. There's a conflagration here. Whack those rumps and lift those knees!

WOMAN II: Fly, fly, Nikodike,
Before they scorch poor Calonike.

WOMAN III: Watch out, lady, they'll burn your drawers. These damned old men with their stupid laws.

WOMAN IV: But maybe, maybe, I've come too late—
The well this morning was in such a state.
Women everywhere drawing water.

WOMAN I: We'll put out the fire and stop the slaughter.
We heard a rumor down by the well
That some old graybeards (on their way to Hell)
Had carried some wood and started a fire.
You know what that is? It's their funeral pyre.

WOMAN V: They threatened to burn these glorious ladies,
But we'll smash them first right down to Hades.

ALL: We've come to aid the goddess,
We'll save her come what may,
The men must never get inside,
We'll keep them from their pay.

WOMAN II: *(she has been grabbed by one of the old men)* Help!! Leave me go, you dog!

WOMAN I: Leave her alone, you simpering corpse.

MAN I: I wouldn't have believed it—an army of women in the Acropolis.

WOMAN I: You scum, you lowest of the low. Male hags, rag bags.

MAN II: This is a sight I never thought to see. A swarm of women buzzing around the Acropolis.

WOMAN II: You're so scared, you'll dirty your pants. But you ain't seen nothing yet.

MAN III: *(stamps his foot)* I will *not* be talked back to by a woman! *(indicating man next to him)* Pick up a log, Phaedrias, and crown her cranium.

WOMAN I: Down with your pots, girls, we'll need both hands in a minute.

MAN I: Give them the old one-two to the jaw, boys, that'll shut 'em up.

WOMAN III: Come on, then. Free shot! *(offers her jaw and one man advances)* Want a kick in the balls? *(he scurries back)*

MAN IV: I'll smash you to pieces with this stick.

WOMAN IV: You just lay a finger on her and you'll never lay anything else again.

MAN IV: Oh yeah?

WOMEN ALL: Yeah.

MAN V: Drop dead.

WOMAN V: I'll rattle your ribs and ravage your rump.

MEN ALL: Euripides! You're right!

MAN VI: "Women are a curse," he said.

WOMAN I: Okay, girls, position your pots. *(they circle the men who bunch together holding their torches in front of them during the following interchange)*

MAN VII: Why the water, you whoremaster's daughter?

WOMAN VI: Why the fire, you walking graveyard? *(turns to the other women, giggling)* It's his funeral pyre!

MAN I: I brought this fire to ignite a pyre and barbecue your friends.

WOMAN VII: I brought this water to put out your fire. What do you think of that?

MAN II: You'll put out my fire?

WOMAN VII: You're not as dumb as you look.

MAN III: Watch it, granny, or I'll fire your fanny.

WOMAN VI: If you've got any soap, I'll give you a bath.

MAN VI: A bath for me? You slut, you.

WOMAN VII: He hasn't used soap since his wedding night!

MAN V: Watch your lip.

WOMAN VII: My lips are free—to say what they like.

MAN I: Burn, lads, burn.

WOMAN I: Soak, girls, soak. *(music stops)*

MEN ALL: Arrrgh!

WOMAN I: Was it too cold? *(the women threaten to pour again)*

MEN ALL: Stop it. Stop it.

WOMAN II: I'm just watering the garden. Maybe you'll sprout a leaf.

MAN II: *(chattering)* I-I-I'm f-f-f-reezing.

WOMAN II: Sorry to have cooled you off, we thought you were in heat. *(the men sit down bedraggled, the women move aside)*

(enter Commissioner and four policemen)

COMMISSIONER: Fire, eh? Females again. Spontaneous combustion of lust. Suspected as much. Rubadubdubbing. Incessant, incontinent whining for wine, ululating for Adonis from the rooftops. Heard it all before. And they do it in the damned parliament! Remember that debate on the Sicilian question? That knucklehead Demostratus rose to propose a naval task force for Sicily. His wife, writhing on the rooftop, stopped him in the middle: "Adonis, oh woe for Adonis." Demostratus, taking his cue from his wife, outshouted her: "A military goddamn draft! Enlist the whole island." She came back at him: "Oh, gnash your teeth and beat your breasts for Adonis." And so, Demostratus—that profane pimple, that son of a boil—rammed his goddamn program through. That's what women are good for: a complete disaster.

MAN I: Save your breath for actual crimes, Commissioner. Look what's happened to us. Insolence, insults, insufferable effrontery, and apart from that, they've soaked us. It looks as though we pissed in our tunics.

COMMISSIONER: By Poseidon, that liquid deity, you got what you deserved. It's all our own fault. We taught them all they know. We are the forgers of fornication. We sowed in them sexual license and now we reap rebellion. You see a husband go into a jeweler's: "Look," he'll say, "remember the necklace you made for my wife? Well, she was having a bit of a ball last night, dancing around, you know, and the prong slipped out of the hole. I've got to go out of town for a few days. Do me a favor, if you've got time. Slip over to the house tonight and put the prong in the hole for her." Someone else will go to the cobbler's—young, but no apprentice, a strong fellow with a great long tool—and say to him: "One of my wife's new sandals is a bit tight. It pinches her right on the pinkie. Could you drop by about lunch time and give it a stretch?" *(shrugs)* What do you expect? This is what happens. . . . *(indicates doors of Acropolis)* Take my own case. I'm the Commissioner for Public Safety. I've got men to pay. I need the money and look what happens. The women have shut *me* out of the public treasury. *(taking command)* All right, men. On your feet. Take up that log over there. Form a line. Get a move on. You can get drunk later. I'll give you a hand. *(They ram the gates without success. After three tries, as they are stepping back, Lysistrata opens the door. Calonike and Myrrhine accompany her.)*

LYSISTRATA: Put that thing down! I'm coming out of my own free will. What we want here is not bolts and bars and locks, but common sense.

COMMISSIONER: Sense? Common sense? You . . . you . . . you . . . Where's a policeman? Arrest her! Tie her hands behind her back.

LYSISTRATA: *(who is carrying wool on a spindle or a knitting needle)* By Artemis, goddess of the hunt, if he touches me, you'll be dropping one man from your payroll. *(Lysistrata jabs him)*

COMMISSIONER: What's this? Retreat? Get back in there. Grab her, the two of you.

MYRRHINE: *(holding a large chamber pot)* By Artemis, goddess of the dew, if you lay a hand on her, I'll kick the shit out of you.

COMMISSIONER: Shit? Disgusting. Arrest her for using obscene language.

CALONIKE: *(carrying a lamp)* By Artemis, goddess of light, if you lay a finger on her, you'll need a doctor.

COMMISSIONER: Apprehend that woman. Get her, NOW!

BOEOTIAN: *(from the roof, with a broom)* By Artemis, goddess of witchcraft, if you go near her, I'll break your head open.

COMMISSIONER: Good God, what a mess. Athens' finest disgraced! Defeated by a gaggle of girls. Close ranks, men! On your marks, get set, CHARGE!

LYSISTRATA: *(holds her hand up and they stop)* Hold it! We've got four battalions of fully equipped infantry women back there.

COMMISSIONER: Go inside and disarm them.

LYSISTRATA: *(gives a loud whistle and women crowd the bottlenecks and the doorway with brooms, pots and pans, etc.)* Attack! Destroy them, you sifters of flour and beaters of eggs, you pressers of garlic, you dough girls, you bar maids, you market militia. Scratch them and tear them, bite and kick. Fall back, don't strip the enemy—the day is ours. *(the policemen are overpowered)*

COMMISSIONER: *(in tears)* Another glorious military victory for Athens!

LYSISTRATA: What did you think we were? There's not an ounce of servility in us. A woman scorned is something to be reckoned with. You underestimated the capacity of freeborn women.

COMMISSIONER: Capacity? I sure as hell did. You'd cause a drought in the saloons if they let you in.

MAN I: Your honor, there's no use talking to animals. I know you're a civil servant, but don't overdo it.

MAN II: Didn't we tell you? They gave us a public bath, fully dressed, without any soap.

WOMAN I: What did you expect, sonny? You made the first move—we made the second. Try it again and you'll get another black eye. *(flute)* We are really sweet little stay-at-homes by nature, all sweetness and light, good little virgins, perfect dolls *(they all rock to and fro coyly)*. But if you stick your finger in a hornet's nest, you're going to get stung.

MEN ALL: *(and drums—they beat their feet rhythmically on the ground)*
Oh Zeus, oh Zeus.
Of all the beasts that thou has wrought,
What monster's worse than woman?
Who shall encompass with his thought
Their endless crimes? Let me tell you ... no man!

They've seized the heights, the rock, the shrine.
But to what end I know not.
There must be *reasons* for the crime *(to audience)*
Do you know why? (pause) I thought not.

MAN I: Scrutinize those women. *Ass*ess their re*butt*als.

MAN II: 'Twould be culpable negligence not to probe this affair to the bottom.

COMMISSIONER: *(as if before a jury)* My first question is this, gentlemen of the ... What possible motive could you have had in seizing the Treasury?

LYSISTRATA: We wanted to keep the money. *No money, no war.*

COMMISSIONER: You think that money is the cause of the war?

LYSISTRATA: Money is the cause of all our problems. Why did Peisander seize the state? Money. Why the coup? Money. But there will be no more excuses. They'll not get another penny.

COMMISSIONER: Then what do you propose to do?

LYSISTRATA: Control the Treasury.

COMMISSIONER: Control the Treasury?

LYSISTRATA: Control the Treasury. National economics and home economics—they're one and the same.

COMMISSIONER: No, they're not.

LYSISTRATA: Why do you say so?

COMMISSIONER: The national economy is for the war effort.

LYSISTRATA: Who needs the war effort?

COMMISSIONER: How can we protect the city?

LYSISTRATA: Leave that to us.

ALL MEN: You?

ALL WOMEN: Us.

COMMISSIONER: God save us.

LYSISTRATA: Leave that to us.

COMMISSIONER: Subversive nonsense!

LYSISTRATA: Why get so upset? There's no stopping us now.

COMMISSIONER: It's a downright crime.

LYSISTRATA: We *must* save you.

COMMISSIONER: *(pouting)* What if I don't want to be saved?

LYSISTRATA: All the more reason to.

COMMISSIONER: Might I ask where you got these ideas of war and peace?

LYSISTRATA: If you'll allow me, I'll tell you.

COMMISSIONER: Out with it then, or I'll ...

LYSISTRATA: Relax and put your hands down.

COMMISSIONER: I can't help myself. You make me so damned angry.

CALONIKE: Watch it.

COMMISSIONER: Watch it yourself, you old wind bag.

LYSISTRATA: Because of our natural self-restraint, we women have tolerated you men ever since this war began. We tolerated you and kept our thoughts to ourselves. (You never let us utter a peep, anyway.) But that does not mean that we were happy with you. We knew you all too well. Very often, in the evening, at suppertime, we would listen to you talk of some enormously important decision you had made. Deep down inside all we felt was pain, but we would force a smile and ask, "How was the assembly today, dear? Did you get to talk about peace?" And my husband would answer, "None of your business. Shut up!" And I would shut up.

CALONIKE: I wouldn't have.

COMMISSIONER: I'd have shut your mouth for you.

LYSISTRATA: But then we would find out that you had passed a more disgusting resolution, and I would ask you, "Darling, how did you manage to do something so absolutely stupid?" And my husband would glare at me and threaten to slap my face if I did not attend to the distaff side of things. And then he'd always quote Homer: "The men must see to the fighting."

COMMISSIONER: Well done. Well done.

LYSISTRATA: What do you mean? Not to let us advise against your idiocy was bad enough, but then again we'd actually hear you out in public saying things like, "Who can we draft? There's not a man left in the country." Someone else would say, "Quite right, not a man left. Pity." And so we women got together and decided to save Greece. There was no time to lose. Therefore, you keep quiet for a change and listen to us. For we have valuable advice to give this country. If you'll listen, we'll put you back on your feet again.

COMMISSIONER: You'll do what? I'm not going to put up with this. I'm not going ...

LYSISTRATA: SILENCE!

COMMISSIONER: I categorically decline to be silent for a woman. Women wear hats.

LYSISTRATA: If that's what is bothering you, try one on and shut up! *(puts one on him)*

CALONIKE: Here's a spindle.

MYRRHINE: And a basket of wool.

CALONIKE: Go on home. There's a sweetheart. Put on your girdle, wind your wool, and mind the beans don't boil over.

LYSISTRATA: "THE WOMEN MUST SEE TO THE FIGHTING."

WOMAN I: Get ready, girls, to dance and sing, it's time to help our friends.

WOMEN ALL: This is a dance that I know well.
My knees shall crack,
Wobble and creak I may, but hell!
I'm ready to attack.
Valor and grace march on ahead,
Love prods us from behind.
Our slogan is "Deny the Bed"
Our purpose: "Save mankind."

WOMAN I: Women, remember your mothers and their mothers before them. What thorns they were in the side of the state. Sting them, Sisters, goad them into submission. You're in full sail.

LYSISTRATA: *(in solemn prayer)*
O Eros of the sweet breath
O Aphrodite, Cyprian Queen,
Breathe the softness of perfume
Upon our breast and thighs.
Tighten and tauten our husbands till they stand erect.
In all of Greece
We shall be called the Peacemakers.

COMMISSIONER: How will you do that?

LYSISTRATA: First we shall make the marketplace off limits to all weapon-crazy soldiers in town.

THEBAN WOMAN: Aphrodite, be praised! Off the streets—and into the bedrooms.

LYSISTRATA: Nowadays there are soldiers in every grocery and pottery shop, clanking around armed to the teeth, like Bacchantes in heat.

COMMISSIONER: Of course, of course, of course. A hero is always prepared.

LYSISTRATA: I suppose he is. But it does look stupid buying sardines in a full suit of armor.

CALONIKE: I saw a captain in the market the other day, all curls and grease—you know the type. He was drinking pea soup out of his helmet!

MYRRHINE: Then there was this huge lunk from Thrace swinging his spear around his head and scaring the woman at the fruit stall. She ran away, she was so scared—and he stole all her figs.

COMMISSIONER: Beside the point, beside the point. Things are in a tangle. How can *you* set them straight?

LYSISTRATA: Simple.

COMMISSIONER: Explain.

LYSISTRATA: Do you know anything about weaving? Say the wool gets tangled. We lift it up, like this, and work out the knots by winding it this way and that, up and down, on the spindles. That's how we'll unravel the war. We'll send our envoys this way and that, up and down, all over Greece.

COMMISSIONER: Wool? Spindles? Are you out of your mind? War is a serious business.

LYSISTRATA: If you had any sense, you'd learn a lesson from women's work.

COMMISSIONER: Prove it.

LYSISTRATA: The first thing we have to do is give the wool a good wash, get the dirt out of the fleece. We beat out the musk and pick out the hickies. Do the same for the city. Lambast the loafers and discard the dodgers. Then our spoiled wool—that's like your job-hunting sycophants—sack the spongers, decapitate the dabblers. But toss together into the wool basket the good aliens, the allies, the strangers, and begin spinning them into a ball. The colonies are loose threads; pick up the ends and gather them in. Wind them all into one, make a great bobbin of yarn, and weave, without bias or seam, a garment of government fit for the people.

COMMISSIONER: It's all very well this weaving and bobbing—when you have absolutely no earthly idea what a war means.

LYSISTRATA: You disgusting excuse for a man! The pain of giving birth was only our first pain. You took our boys and sent *them to their deaths in Sicily.*

COMMISSIONER: Quiet! I beg you, let that memory lie still.

LYSISTRATA: And now, when youth and beauty are still with us and our blood is hot, you take our husbands away, and we sleep alone. That's bad enough for us married women. But I pity the virgins growing old, alone in their beds.

COMMISSIONER: Well, men grow old too, you know.

LYSISTRATA: But it's not the same. A soldier's discharged, bald as a coot he may be, and ... zap! he marries a nymphette. But a woman only has one summer, and when that has slipped by, she can spend her days and her years consulting oracles and fortune tellers, but they'll never send her a husband.

COMMISSIONER: *(preening himself and offering his service)* But if a man can ... er ... rise to the occasion....

LYSISTRATA: Rise? Rise? Lie down and die. *(they attack him)* Go buy a coffin. I'll bake a funeral cake. Here, take this garland. *(winds wool around him)*

MYRRHINE: *(empties chamber pot)* Accept this token of our grief.

CALONIKE: And a final garland for the dead. *(bangs him on the head with the lamp)*

LYSISTRATA: What are you waiting for? The boats afloat? Charon's waiting, you're holding up the boat for hell.

COMMISSIONER: This is scandalous—maltreatment of a public official—maltreatment of ME! *(departing)* I must show my fellow commissioners what you have done. I'm soaked.

LYSISTRATA: We should have given him the last rites. Come back tomorrow, Commissioner, we'll lay you out.

MAN I: Arise, ye men of Athens, fight for your freedom. Now. *(they take off their cloaks)*

MEN ALL: There's something rotten in the state of Athens.
An ominous aroma of constitutional rot.
My nose can smell a radical dissenter,
An anarchist, tyrannous, feminist plot.

The Spartans are behind it.
They must have masterminded
This anarchist, tyrannous, feminist plot.

MAN II: And *Cleisthenes*, our local queen, *he's* the double agent.

MEN ALL: So fight them, stop them, hold them, Brothers.
They're our wives, our sisters, our mothers.
They've sold us out; the streets are teeming with women of all ages.
Shall we stand by and let them confiscate our wages?

MAN I: Should *women* tell soldiers what to do? *Women* drilling us about our helmets and shields. *Women,* can you believe it, telling us to trust the nice little Spartans and put our heads in the mouth of the wolf. Tyranny, that's what it is. But not over me! I'll use their own weapon against them. With knife under cloak I'll take my post in the marketplace beside the statues of our national heroes—Harmodius, and Aristogiton, and Me. Striking an epic pose, so, with full approval of the gods above. Pow, here's a punch in the jaw.

WOMAN I: Your mommy won't recognize you when you get home. *(they take off their cloaks)* Okay, girls, take it off, take it all off. Now listen to me, *audience*, and fathom what we say. We women love this country, too. It isn't only you.

WOMEN ALL: When I was seven and sweet and young,
I carried flowers for the gods.
At ten years old, I danced and sung,
And then in saffron robes I walked, the bearer of the holy basket.
And then to cap this proud progression
I led the whole procession at Athena's celebration.

A virgin beauty, proud of her nation.

WOMAN II: So don't you think I want to do all I can for Athens? I'm giving Athens the best advice she ever had. Don't I pay taxes to the state? Yes, I pay them in baby boys. And what do you contribute, you impotent scum? Absolutely nothing. All our revenue gone, rifled. And not a penny out of your pockets. Well, then? Can you cough up an answer to that? So you're the ones who better watch out or—pow, here's a punch in the jaw.

MEN ALL: Their native respect for our manhood is small
And keeps getting smaller. Let's bottle their gall.
The man who won't battle has no balls at all.

Let's loosen our belts and tighten our fists.
We'll show them our manhood and what they have missed.

A century back we soared to the heights
And beat vile tyranny down.
'Tis time again to show our strength
And win us world renown.

MAN I: Give them an inch and they'll take a mile. They'll be building ships next and planning new battles.

MAN II: Maybe they want to get involved in the cavalry. They like a good ride. Just pop down to the temple, you'll see paintings of Amazons wrestling with all those men.

MAN III: So watch it, ladies, or we'll put you in your place—in the stocks.

WOMEN ALL: The beast in me is fit for a brawl.

Just rile me a bit and I'll kick down the wall.
You'll bawl to your friends that you've no balls at
all.

Let's loosen our belts and give 'em a sniff
Of feminine fury and not just a whiff.

Tangle with me and you'll get cramps.
I'll break your neck, you aging Gramps,
I'll scramble your eggs
And bake your beans.
Between my legs
You'll see such scenes
That never in your life did you think you'd see.
I'm tough—that's me.

WOMAN II: If Lampito is on my side and Ismenia, you can go to hell. Pass a law. Pass seven. Make a reputation for yourself, worse than the one you've got now.

WOMAN III: I wanted one of those Boeotian eels for a party yesterday. Couldn't get one anywhere. Why? You'd outlawed the eels.

WOMAN II: Brilliant.

WOMAN III: So watch it, bring your neck over here and I'll break it! *(they chase the men off the stage)*

Several days have elapsed.

WOMAN I: *(mock tragic)* Mistress, queen of this our subtle scheme, why dost thou come forth thus sorrowful?

LYSISTRATA: Oh, wickedness of women! The female mind doth sap my soul and set my feet a-pacing.

WOMAN I: What dost thou say? What dost thou say?

LYSISTRATA: The truth! The truth!

WOMAN I: What woe is this? Declare to us your friends.

LYSISTRATA: 'Tis a shame to utter, a pain to keep unsaid.

WOMAN I: Conceal not the affliction which is ours.

LYSISTRATA: *(breaking the mock tragedy)* Okay! We wanna get laid! That's the long and short of it.

WOMAN I: Oh, my god.

LYSISTRATA: No, not by God. It's men they want. MEN! I can't keep them away from men. They're all trying to get out of here. I saw one just five minutes ago crawling out through the sewerhole over in Pan's Cave. And there was another one swinging down on a rope and tackle. Last night I saw a woman mount a sparrow, all ready to go off and join a whorehouse, but luckily I grabbed her by the hair. And all the excuses you'd ever want to hear to get out and go home. Here's one now. Hey, you, where do you think you're going?

WOMAN I: I'll be right back, I promise you. Just let me give it a good stretch on the bed.

LYSISTRATA: No stretching. No bedding. And no going nowhere.

WOMAN I: But my wool will be ruined.

LYSISTRATA: Tough. Get back in there.

WOMAN II: What a shame. What a shame. I'm so *worried* about my flax. I left it at home, poor thing, totally unstripped.

LYSISTRATA: She's worried about her flax. Get inside.

WOMAN II: But I *will* come back, I swear. I'll just strip it, pluck a few fibers, and be right back.

LYSISTRATA: No stripping, no plucking. Get back in there. Once you let one do it, they'll all want to.

WOMAN III: O goddess of childbirth, let me not deliver in this sacred precinct.

LYSISTRATA: What nonsense is this?

WOMAN III: My contractions have started.

LYSISTRATA: Contractions? You weren't even pregnant yesterday.

WOMAN III: But I am today. Isn't it exciting? Quick, I must go home and get a midwife.

LYSISTRATA: What are you talking about? What's this hard lump you've got?

WOMAN III: *(coyly)* A little baby boy.

LYSISTRATA: This? It's hollow. And sounds like it's

made of brass. Come off it. Drop it. It's Athena's helmet. You took it off the statue. Pregnant! You...

WOMAN III: I am *so* pregnant.

LYSISTRATA: Then what's the helmet for?

WOMAN III: If my little chickie's born here, in the Acropolis, I'll pop him inside like a little birdie's nest.

LYSISTRATA: Get out of here. I'll call you when we've given your helmet a name.

WOMAN III: But I can't stay in the Acropolis. Last night I dreamed I saw the sacred snake.

WOMAN II: And the owls up there! I can't sleep a wink.

LYSISTRATA: Stop lying to me. What you want is your men. But don't think *they* don't want you. Their nights are hard, I can tell you. If you can last a little longer, we shall win. The oracle says so.

WOMAN II: Oracle, what oracle? Tell us.

LYSISTRATA: This is what it says:
When swallows shall the hoopoe shun
And spurn his hot desire,
Zeus will perfect what they've begun
And set the lower higher.

WOMAN I: That means we'll have to do it on top of them.

LYSISTRATA: But if the swallows shall fall out
And take the hoopoe's bait,
A curse must mark their hour of doubt
And infamy seal their fate.

WOMAN III: There's nothing obscure about *that* oracle. Yeech.

LYSISTRATA: Come, let's not give in to our desires. Let's go back in. We could never live down the disgrace of betraying the oracle. Come back inside.

CHORUS OF MEN

MEN ALL: Now,
I have a little story
That I heard when I was a boy,
How
The huntsman, bold Melanion, was once a harried quarry.
The women in town, tracked him down, and badgered him to marry.
Melanion knew the cornered male eventually cohabits;
Assessing the odds, he took to the woods, and lived by trapping rabbits.
He remained a virgin, long sustained by rabbit meat and hate,
And never returned, but ever remained an absolute celibate.
Melanion is our ideal; his loathing makes us free.
Our constant aim is the gem-like flame of his misogyny.

MAN IV: Gimme a kiss, hag face.

WOMAN IV: Want an onion in your eye?

MAN IV: How about a kick?

WOMAN IV: What a thatch! What a jungle.

MEN ALL: It's a sign of manhood!

CHORUS OF WOMEN

WOMEN ALL: Now,
I will tell you a story
To counter your Melanion,
How
Timon, the noted local grump, spent his life in a rage,
A cantankerous hairy lump, the bane of the men of his age.
When random contracts overtaxed him, he didn't stop to pack,
But loaded curses on the male of the species, left town, and never came back.
Timon, you see, was a misanthrope in a properly narrow sense.
His spleen was vented only on *men*; *we* were his dearest friends.

WOMAN V: How about a punch in the mouth?

MAN V: I'm not afraid of you.

WOMAN V: How about a kick?

MAN V: She showed me her mantrap.

WOMEN ALL: It's a sign of womanhood.

LYSISTRATA: Quick, quick. Everyone. Over here!

WOMAN I: What's all the fuss about?

LYSISTRATA: It's a man, a real man, simply bulging with love. O, Aphrodite, goddess, show us the right road.

WOMAN II: Where is he?

LYSISTRATA: Over there on the steps.

WOMAN III: You're right, you're right. But who is he?

LYSISTRATA: Do any of you know him?

MYRRHINE: It's my husband, Kinesias.

LYSISTRATA: Your duty is clear. Tease him and taunt him. Forbid it and flaunt it. Do everything except the one thing we swore we wouldn't.

MYRRHINE: Don't worry, leave him to me.

LYSISTRATA: I'll help you get him started. I'll stay here. The rest of you get back in.

KINESIAS: Oh God, oh my God, it's agony. Hyperextension! The rack and the rod.

LYSISTRATA: Who goes there? Who penetrates our positions?

KINESIAS: Me.

LYSISTRATA: A man?

KINESIAS: Can't you see?

LYSISTRATA: Then get right out of here.

KINESIAS: Who are you to be throwing me out?

LYSISTRATA: The watch guard.

KINESIAS: Officer, please, by all the gods, bring Myrrhine out here.

LYSISTRATA: Myrrhine? And who, sir, are you?

KINESIAS: Name's Kinesias. My friends call me Humper. I'm her husband.

LYSISTRATA: Oh, I beg your pardon. Of course. We're glad to see you. I've heard so much about you. Myrrhine, the sweetheart, is always talking about Kinesias. Never nibbles an egg or sucks a fig without saying, "Here's to Kinesias."

KINESIAS: Is that the truth?

LYSISTRATA: It is. When we're discussing men, she always says, "Compared with Kinesias, the rest have nothing."

KINESIAS: BRING HER OUT HERE.

LYSISTRATA: And what do I get out of it?

KINESIAS: You see how it is. I'll raise whatever I can. How about *this*?

LYSISTRATA: I'll give her a call.

KINESIAS: Hurry, hurry. She left our house and happiness went with her. Now I live with pain in an empty home, eating that awful tasteless food. IT'S HARD!

MYRRHINE: Oh, I do love him, I'm mad about him. But he doesn't want my love. Please don't make me see him.

KINESIAS: Myrrhine, Myrrhine, darling. What do you mean, not love you? Come down here.

MYRRHINE: Down there? Certainly not.

KINESIAS: It's me, Myrrhine. I'm begging you. Please come down.

MYRRHINE: I don't see why you're begging me. You don't need me.

KINESIAS: Not need you? I'm at the end of my rope.

MYRRHINE: I'm leaving.

KINESIAS: No, wait. For the sake of the child. Hey you little ... call your mother.

BABY: Mama, Mama.

KINESIAS: Haven't you any feeling? He hasn't been washed and fed for a week.

MYRRHINE: Oh, my baby, your father is so cruel to you.

KINESIAS: Then come down and get him.

MYRRHINE: Oh, all right. Motherhood! I'll have to come. I've got no choice.

KINESIAS: She looks younger and prettier. And when she's mad like that and her eyes flash, I just go crazy with desire.

MYRRHINE: Sweet babykins, with such a nasty daddy. Give mommy a kiss. Num num num num num.

KINESIAS: You should be ashamed of yourself, letting those women lead you around. Why do you do these things? It's bad for both of us.

MYRRHINE: Keep your hands off me.

KINESIAS: Our house is a disaster.

MYRRHINE: I don't care.

KINESIAS: But your weaving is in a mess—the loom is full of chickens.

MYRRHINE: I don't give a damn.

KINESIAS: And the holy rites of Aphrodite? Think how long that's been. Come on, darling, let's go home.

MYRRHINE: I absolutely refuse—unless you agree to a truce to end the war.

KINESIAS: All right, then. All right, then, we'll stop the war.

MYRRHINE: If you do it, I'll do it. For the time being, I've sworn off.

KINESIAS: Lie down for just a minute.

MYRRHINE: Stop it! No! But that doesn't mean that I don't love you.

KINESIAS: I know you do, darling Myrrhine. So LIE DOWN.

MYRRHINE: Don't be disgusting. In front of the baby?

KINESIAS: Of course not. Take this thing home, nurse. Well, darling, we're rid of the kid. Let's go to bed.

MYRRHINE: Where does one do this sort of thing?

KINESIAS: Where? Pan's Cave will be perfect.

MYRRHINE: But what about my purification after we do it? I need it to get back in.

KINESIAS: Sponge off in the pool next door.

MYRRHINE: I did swear an oath, you know. Should I perjure myself?

KINESIAS: Forget the oath. I'll take the consequences.

MYRRHINE: I'll go get us a bed.

KINESIAS: No! No bed. The ground's good enough for us.

MYRRHINE: *You*, on the dirty ground? Darling, I'd never let you.

KINESIAS: Oh, she loves me, she really must love me.

MYRRHINE: Here's the bed. Now get into bed while I undress. Oh dear! There's no mattress.

KINESIAS: I don't want a mattress.

MYRRHINE: You can't sleep without a mattress.

KINESIAS: Give me a kiss, then.

MYRRHINE: *(bites his neck)* There.

KINESIAS: Ow! Come back quick. Hurry.

MYRRHINE: Here's the mattress. Now, into bed while I undress. Wait a minute. I forgot the pillow.

KINESIAS: I don't want a pillow!

MYRRHINE: I know, but *I* do.

KINESIAS: I'll burst, God knows, I'll burst.

MYRRHINE: There we are. Ups-a-daisy.

KINESIAS: So we are, so we are. Come here, my little jewel box.

MYRRHINE: Just taking off my girdle. Don't break your promise: no cheating about the peace.

KINESIAS: I swear to God. I'll die first.

MYRRHINE: Just look, there isn't a sheet.

KINESIAS: I don't want a sheet. I want to get laid.

MYRRHINE: You'll get what you want. I'll be right back.

KINESIAS: The woman will kill me with her pillows and sheets.

MYRRHINE: Here we are. Get up.

KINESIAS: Up? I've been up for weeks.

MYRRHINE: Would you like a dash of perfume?

KINESIAS: No, I damn well would not.

MYRRHINE: Well, you're damn well going to get some anyway.

KINESIAS: Dear Zeus, Lord, I don't ask for much. But please make her spill the bottle.

MYRRHINE: Hold out your hand like a good boy. Rub it right in.

KINESIAS: Damn it, it smells terrible. It's turning me off, not on.

MYRRHINE: Silly me. I brought the wrong bottle. This is the Rhodian brand.

KINESIAS: It's fine, it's lovely, leave it alone.

MYRRHINE: No trouble at all! Now, don't go away.

KINESIAS: Goddamn the man who invented perfume.

MYRRHINE: Here, try this bottle.

KINESIAS: No, you try mine. Come to bed, you witch.... And don't bring me anything else.

MYRRHINE: That's the last thing you're getting. Let me just take my shoes off. Incidentally, you will remember to vote for the truce.

KINESIAS: I'll think it over! *(Myrrhine runs away)* God in heaven, she's gone. She's left me standing, stiff as a board. *(mock tragedy, to his phallus)* We're left alone, abandoned by the most beautiful woman in the world! There's the rub. To a nunnery, come? *(breaking the mock tragedy)* I know a marvelous little brothel down the street....

CHORUS OF OLD MEN

MEN ALL: *(mock tragedy)*
Alas for the woes of man, alas.

She hath brought you to a pretty pass.
Split, heart. Proud spirit, crack.
Sag, flesh, and cock, go slack.

MAN VI: Your morning lay.

MAN VII: Has gone astray.

KINESIAS: O Zeus, reduce the throbs, the throes.

MAN I: Friend, 'twas she that brought you to this state,
That hag, that bag, that reprobate.

KINESIAS: *(departing)* No, curse not my light of love, my dove, my sweet.

MEN ALL: Sweet? Oh blessed Zeus who rul'st the sky,
Snatch these women up on high,
Spin them all into one great ball
And then from the heavens let them fall.
Down they'll come, the pretty dears,
And split themselves on our thick spears.

(enter Spartan herald)

SPARTAN: Excuse me, could you direct me to the Central Committee? I have something to show them.

COMMISSIONER: Are you a man or a fertility symbol?

SPARTAN: I refuse to answer that question. I, sir, am an official herald from Sparta, and I have come to talk about an armistice.

COMMISSIONER: Then, why are you carrying that spear under your cloak?

SPARTAN: That, sir, is not a spear.

COMMISSIONER: Then take the cucumber out of your pocket.

SPARTAN: You, sir, are out of your mind.

COMMISSIONER: You have a hernia, maybe?

SPARTAN: I have business to attend to.

COMMISSIONER: Well, something's up, I can see that. And I don't like it.

SPARTAN: Sir, I resent this.

COMMISSIONER: I see that. But what *is* it?

SPARTAN: It's a rod of office. I told you I am an official herald from Sparta.

COMMISSIONER: That's some rod of office. But tell me, how are things in Sparta?

SPARTAN: Hard, sir, hard. We're at a standstill. Can't seem to think of anything but women.

COMMISSIONER: That certainly is a coincidence. Tell me, who do you think is behind this? Has Pan put a jinx on you?

SPARTAN: Pan? Good God, no.... It's Lampito and her little nudie girl friends. They won't let anyone near them.

COMMISSIONER: How are you handling it?

SPARTAN: We're going out of our minds, if you want to know the truth. Everyone's walking around hunched over like this, like men carrying candles in a gale. The women have sworn that they will have nothing to do with us until we make a treaty.

COMMISSIONER: I know. There's a general uprising all over Greece. But go back to Sparta, see that they send an armistice delegation. I'll work on things on this end. I can safely say that I too am a man of good standing. They'll listen to me.

SPARTAN: You're a man after my own heart, sir. I thank you.

MAN I: The female of the species is deadlier than the male. An animal is all she is, a creature without shame.

WOMAN I: Then why do you fight us? Why do you attack? We might have been your partners, and worked behind your back.

MAN II: I'll never stop hating you.

WOMAN II: As you wish, but please get dressed. You look so stupid. Come on, get into your cloak. *(women all dress their counterparts)*

MAN III: Thank you. I must admit I stripped it off in anger.

WOMAN III: That's better. Now you look like a man again. Why have you been so unpleasant?

WOMAN IV: Look, there's an insect in your eye. Shall I take it out?

MAN IV: So that's what it was, a damn mosquito. Yes, please take it out.

WOMAN V: I will, but please learn to behave, and you must treat us better.

WOMAN VI: Good God, what a size! A veritable monster. A dragonfly.

MAN VI: Oh, what a relief, your kindness pleases. But now you've unplugged me, here come the tears.

WOMAN VI: I'll dry your tears, though I can't say why. You've behaved so badly.

WOMEN ALL: And now, one little kiss!

MEN ALL: No you don't.

WOMEN ALL: Yes we will.

MEN ALL: Just one. *(they kiss)*

MAN I: How you get around us! There never was a truer saying!

MEN ALL: Impossible to live with you; impossible without.

WOMAN I: Then let us sign a mutual treaty. And never again will we raise a voice or hand in anger. Let's make a single chorus and celebrate our joy.

JOINT CHORUS ALL:

Let it never be said
That my tongue is malicious.
Both by word and by deed
We shall be noble and gracious.

MAN I: There's misery enough.

WOMAN I: There's misery enough.

CHORUS ALL: *(to audience)*

Is there anyone here who would like a small loan?
My purse is crammed—as you'll soon find—
And you needn't pay me back till peace gets signed.

We've organized a dinner for some playboys from Carystos.
A lovely soup, a piglet roasted brown,
And then for all of you, some wine to wash it down.

MAN I: You're all coming, I hope.

WOMAN I: Bring the children.

CHORUS ALL:

But take a bath and then come over.
Walk right up, as if you owned the place.
I'm sure you'll never grudge it, if
you find you cannot budge it, if
the door is BOLTED IN YOUR FACE.

MAN I: Look at this lot! It's the commissioners from Sparta. Look at the way they're walking. Gentlemen, welcome to Athens. How is life in Sparta?

SPARTAN I: Do we have to tell you? Can't you see what a state we're in?

MAN II: Well, I'll be damned, a disaster area.

SPARTAN II: It's beyond belief. But come, gentlemen, call in your commissioners and let's talk about peace.

MAN III: It's the same here at Athens. None of the men can bear to wear anything below the waist. It's a kind of pelvic paralysis. *(enter Commissioner and Kinesias)*

COMMISSIONER: Somebody call Lysistrata. It looks like we're all in the same state.

SPARTAN I: It's a dreadful situation. Do you feel a certain strain in the morning? What do you do about it?

KINESIAS: I do, sir, and I take whatever is handy. But a few more days and Cleisthenes had better watch himself.

COMMISSIONER: Could I give you a bit of advice? Try and hide your condition. You know what they did to those statues of Hermes. Once bitten, twice shy.

SPARTANS I AND II: *(covering their phalluses)* Thank you very much!

KINESIAS: Anyway, welcome, gentlemen—despite the seriousness of the situation.

SPARTAN I: It could be worse. If those Hermes choppers had seen us, they might have taken us down a peg or two.

COMMISSIONER: Let's get down to details. Men of Sparta, what is your proposal?

SPARTAN II: We propose to consider peace.

COMMISSIONER: Excellent. That is also our intention. Call Lysistrata. There will be no peace without her.

SPARTAN I: Call Lysis—anybody, only hurry.

KINESIAS: There's no need to call. Here she is. She must have heard us talking.

MAN I: Hail, Lysistrata, most virile of women. Now in your hour of greatness you must be terrible in your might.

MAN II: Be tender.

MAN III: Be lofty.

MAN IV: Be lowbrow.

MAN V: Be severe.

MAN VI: Be demure.

WOMAN I: You hold the leading statesmen of this land
In the palm of your beautiful hand.
We entrust to you our common fate. It is yours to decide the future of Greece.

LYSISTRATA: That will not be difficult (unless you

start taking each other to bed—but I'd soon find out about that). Where's Reconciliation? *(Reconciliation—a scantily clad woman—enters)* No, dear, not like our husbands—be a gentlewoman. If they refuse their hands, take 'em by the handle. Now do the same for the Athenians. Take anything they've got to offer. Stand there, please. And you over here. Now all of you listen to me. I am only a woman, I know. But I've a mind—and not a bad one. I was born with it. And I listened to my father and my elders. My education was not entirely worthless. Well, now that I've got you here, I intend to give you hell. At festivals, in Pan-Hellenic harmony, like true blood brothers, you share the self-same basin of holy water. You share altars all over Greece—Thermopylae, Olympia, Delphi. But now when Persia sits by and waits, you men go raiding through the country from both sides. Greek killing Greek. That is my first point.

ATHENIAN: Let me get at you, you lovely thing, you.

LYSISTRATA: Men of Sparta, I direct these remarks to you. Have you forgotten that Pericleides came from your country once to ask our help? I can see him now, his grey face, his somber gown. Messene was up in arms against you. You needed an army. And Kimon took out four thousand troops from Athens—an army which saved the state of Sparta. Yet every spring now, you come and decimate our crops.

ATHENIAN: The Spartans are clearly in the wrong.

SPARTAN I: We were wrong, but that's the prettiest behind I ever saw.

LYSISTRATA: And you, Athenians, do you think I've nothing to say to you? Have you forgotten how the Spartans saved us in our hour of need? Their army destroyed the Thessalians and Hippias and his friends. That was Sparta and only Sparta that saved Athens from slavery.

SPARTAN I: What a figure of speech!

ATHENIAN: What a conjunction!

LYSISTRATA: Then why are we fighting? After all this mutual assistance in the past?

SPARTAN I: We are ready, madam. First, that place you have in the rear.

LYSISTRATA: What place?

SPARTAN I: I mean the region of Pylos, ma'am.

COMMISSIONER: Not a chance, by God.

LYSISTRATA: Give it to them.

COMMISSIONER: But what shall we have to bargain with?

LYSISTRATA: Ask for something else in exchange.

COMMISSIONER: All right. *(using Reconciliation as a map)* We'll give you Pylos in the rear, if you give us . . . the twin peaks . . . the Corinthian Delta . . . and the Legs of Megara.

SPARTAN I: My government objects.

LYSISTRATA: Overruled. What's a pair of legs?

KINESIAS: I feel an urgent desire to plow a few furrows.

SPARTAN II: A little fertilizer first, before I sow my seed.

LYSISTRATA: The country life is yours once you've made peace. If you are serious, consult your respective leaders and your allies.

ATHENIAN: What do you mean, allies? We have here a mutual problem of postponed copulation. WE ARE WASTING TIME.

SPARTAN I: My government agrees. *(general rejoicing)*

LYSISTRATA: Then attend to your purification and we, the women, will entertain you in the citadel and treat you to all the delights of a home-cooked banquet. You'll exchange your oaths and pledge your faith, and every man will take his wife and depart for home. *(she exits)*

KINESIAS: Let's get it over with.

SPARTAN I: Lead the way.

KINESIAS: Come on, let's go, hurry. *(all exit)*

CHORUS OF WOMEN

WOMEN ALL: *(during song they throw nuts to the audience)*
I'm so happy at the way things went.
I'm feeling quite lightheaded.
I'll hand to you whatever you want,
Whatever you want, whatever you want.
Embroidery fine and ornaments bright,
Delight of young girls in the prime of their life.
Come over to my house and sample my wine.
It's there for the taking; the drinking is free,
Yes, come over to my house
(But you'll find nothing there),
Bring all of the family, all your kids and your aunts,
I'll feed you and stuff you and go the whole hog,
But don't come too close, we've got a big savage dog.

CHORUS OF MEN

MAN I: Come on, let me in.

COMMISSIONER: *(opens the door; he is holding a torch)* Move along there now. Get a move on. I'd burn your ass for you if it wasn't such an old joke. But I refuse to do it. *(looks at audience)* All right, if that's what you want....

MEN ALL: We shall not be moved.

COMMISSIONER: Get away from here. The gentlemen from Sparta are just coming back from dinner.

SPARTAN II: I must say, I've never seen such a spread.

COMMISSIONER: Those Spartans were absolutely marvelous. And why not? A sober man is a fool. Men of Athens, mark my words, the only good ambassador is a drunken ambassador. When in Sparta we're sober—they make speeches, we shut our ears. It's useless. But today we made music together. It was harmony and peace in there. *(sees the chorus)* Get out of here.

SPARTAN I: I beg you, madam, would you play for us upon your flute? We would like to sing a song in honor of Athens. *(Men's Chorus remove their masks and join him)*

MEN ALL: Memory ... Send me ... Your Muse ... Who Knows ... Our glory ... Knows Athens ... Tell the story ... At Artemisium ... Like gods they stampeded ... the hulks of the Medes ... And Leonidas ... leading us ... and flowed ... down our cheeks ... to our knees below ... The

Persians there ... like the sands of the sea ... Hither, huntress ... virgin, goddess ... tracker, slayer ... to our truce! ... Hold us ever ... fast together ... bring our pledges ... love and increase ... wean us from the fox's wiles ... Hither, huntress ... Virgin, hither ...

LYSISTRATA: Now all is well, all is well. Spartans, take your wives. Athenians, take your wives. Live in union, in conjugal bliss. May we never again make wars in the world.

DOUBLE CHORUS:
Start the chorus dancing,
Summon all the graces,
Artemis, dance, dance Phoebus, Lord of Dancing, dance.
Call on Bacchus, whirl the Thyrsus, dance Lady Hera, dance.
Call the flashing fiery Zeus,
Call the gods, call all the gods,
Dance for the dearest bringer of peace, glorious Aphrodite.

Ai Ai Ai Ai
Leap for victory.

Ai Ai Ai Ai
Hail Hail Hail.

LYSISTRATA: Spartan, sing for us again.

SPARTAN I: From Taygetos, from Taygetos,
Spartan muse, come down,
Sing to the lord Apollo
Who rules Amyklai Town.
Dance for Leda's twins, dance for Helen of Troy,

Dance for the girls and the joy of the whirls of
their curls
And the joy of their feet as they prance.
Leap like a deer and sing; Glory Athena, glory
Athena, glory Athena,
Peace, peace, peace, peace, peace.